JANE EYRE

David Malouf is internationally recognised as one of Australia's finest contemporary writers. His novels include *Remembering Babylon,* shortlisted for the 1993 Booker Prize and winner of the first IMPAC Dublin Literary Award, and *The Great World,* winner of both the Commonwealth Writer's Prize and the Prix Fémina Etranger in 1991. He has also published collections of poetry and a volume of autobiography. He lives in Sydney.

David Malouf

JANE EYRE

V

VINTAGE

Published by Vintage 2000

2 4 6 8 10 9 7 5 3

Copyright © David Malouf 2000

First published in Great Britain by Vintage 2000

Vintage
Random House, 20 Vauxhall Bridge Road, London SW1V
2SA

Random House Australia (Pty) Limited
20 Alfred Street, Milsons Point, Sydney,
New South Wales 2061, Australia

Random House New Zealand Limited
18 Poland Road, Glenfield,
Auckland 10, New Zealand

Random House (Pty) Limited
Endulini, 5A Jubilee Road, Parktown 2193, South Africa

The Random House Group Limited Reg. No. 954009
www.randomhouse.co.uk

A CIP catalogue record for this book
is available from the British Library

ISBN 0 09 9286262

Printed and bound in Great Britain by Clays Ltd, St Ives PLC

Set in 10½/12 Sabon by SX Composing DTP, Rayleigh,
Essex

The Random House Group Limited supports The Forest Stewardship
Council (FSC®), the leading international forest certification organisation.
Our books carrying the FSC label are printed on FSC® certified paper.
FSC is the only forest certification scheme endorsed by the leading
environmental organisations, including Greenpeace. Our
paper procurement policy can be found at
www.randomhouse.co.uk/environment

Dramatis Personae

Jane Eyre .... Soprano
Adele .... Girl Soprano
Mrs Fairfax .... Mezzo Soprano
Mrs Rochester .... Contralto
Mr Rochester .... Baritone

INTRODUCTION

One hundred and fifty years after it was first published, Charlotte Brontë's *Jane Eyre* is the most widely read and widely translated novel in the English language, a fact that would astonish its earliest readers for whom its subject seemed objectionable and its telling crude and overwrought. One reason, surely, is that the central situation seems to us to touch on so many areas of experience, only half open then, or suggestively closed – like the row of doors that made the upper storey at Thornfield, for Jane, 'like a corridor in some Bluebeard's castle,' – that have now been thrown open to reveal not their final secrets, but a whole set of further questions and mysteries – questions about female sexuality and the patterns of feminine rebelliousness and submission; about colonial exploitation, and the lure, but also the fear, of the exotic, to name just a few of the issues that are alive and contemporary in the book and have in these last years been taken up for further exploitation, either in fiction, trashy or otherwise, or as subjects for socio-critical analysis.

So much for the intellectual legacy of *Jane Eyre*, which is rich enough. But none of that accounts for the hold the book has on our imagination, for the sense we have of being haunted by it as Jane is, after she has left

Thornfield, by the house and its atmosphere and by the 'ghost' of Mr Rochester. That too has to do with a voice – Jane's voice as narrator, one of the most intimate and compelling in all fiction, and with Jane's own sense that the story she is telling, with its echoes of *Bluebeard* and *The Demon Lover* and *Beauty and the Beast*, is itself a fable, with something of the shape and archetypal glow of fairytale. A young girl, orphaned, plain, sensible, and almost entirely without fear, sets out to uncover the mysteries of the house she has come to, and through a special sympathy, finds, under the rough exterior of a man who has been wounded and cast out of society, the gentler lineaments of a lover – not quite a prince charming but, just as he is, her one true love. They are of one nature, Jane and Mr Rochester. As she tells us, setting him against all others, and against all the opposing circumstances of age, wealth, position: 'He is not of their kind; I believe he is of mine; I am sure he is, – I feel akin to him, – I understand the language of his countenance and movements; though rank and wealth sever us widely, I have something in my brain and heart, in my blood and veins, that assimilates me mentally to him.'

It is the voice of the narrator in *Jane Eyre* that holds the book together and holds us too; commands our attention and inward consent, engages our emotions, convinces us, however improbable the events and the turn of events it is recounting, that the world of the novel is our own, as close to us as our own breath.

This intimacy, this quality of a spell cast over us, is a large part of what we recall as the book's special atmosphere. For lovers of *Jane Eyre*, the very first sentence, 'There was no possibility of taking a walk that day', with all it holds of what is to come, is like the opening of a magic formula whose unfolding in our head as we read is Jane's voice and the *book*. What any dramatisation of *Jane Eyre* must find is an equivalent for that voice, something that will engage us with the same intimacy, catch us in the same web of enchantment.

Jane Eyre, the libretto, begins with Jane herself when she has already left Thornfield and its temptations. She is, as in the book, the narrator, haunted by voices that are the embodiment in her head of Thornfield and its surroundings and of those there who still have a hold on her heart. She resists them. What she wants is quietness, solitude. But in recalling the past she feels it come alive in her. In beginning to retell the events at Thornfield she finds herself drawn back to a place that in spirit she has never left, knocking at the same door, once again taking up a story whose pull on her emotions is irresistible.

I have always felt that in any action that presents itself as a subject of opera there should be an element that for its fullest expression *demands* music rather than simply tolerating it. The voice of Mr Rochester calling to Jane out of the night, which is perhaps the strongest memory we carry away from the book, the strangest, the most romantic, seems to me to offer such an essentially *musical* possibility. Music makes its own space. Voices meet and join there, whatever the real distance between them. Jane can be, at one moment, inside the house, questioning herself about how the spirit of its absent master may be found among his possessions, and in the next, with just a few bars of musical transition, outside on the ice, with Mr Rochester's horse rearing above her.

The opera begins with those voices from the

past calling in Jane's head. It moves to its climax when Jane realises that the voice she hears so insistently calling 'Jane, Jane' belongs to the present and is real, having travelled across many miles to find her and make its passionate appeal. The opera is the unfolding in Jane's memory of the events at Thornfield, but, as we see it, in real space and real time. Its movement is from Jane's belief that the voice of Mr Rochester is a projection of her own painful yearning to the discovery that it is the voice of her lover's present need for her – one that only she can fill.

I should say at once that some of what, as readers of Charlotte Brontë, we love the best in the book, Jane's ordeal in the red room and her defiance of Mrs Reed, her schooldays at Lowood, Mrs Reed's death, Jane's extraordinary period after she has fled from Thornfield as a tramp woman on the moors – marvellous passages that give richness and complexity to the story – will not be found here. My task as a librettist was to produce a piece with a single action and for no more than five voices, though I might add that the increase in tension that this produces seems to me to be an advantage rather than a limitation. I have used only what, in its teasing suggestion and unsettling reverberations, has most deeply impressed a century and a half of readers, the triangular relationship between Jane, Edward Rochester and the mysterious woman in the attic, and have made that a re-enactment in Jane's head. The present psychodrama, a concentration of the central action of the book, is Jane's story interiorised, experienced with the kind of dreamlike intensity that belongs to that inner world where even the most ordinary events have the shape of the myth.

A word, finally, about language.

The language of opera, if it is to be heard, must be transparent rather than dense; striking if possible, memorable certainly, straightforward both in structure and meaning; it must not draw attention to itself in such a way as to draw attention *away* from the music. It is the music, finally, that will determine pace and emotion. It is in the dimension of music that drama will be created, with all that means of tension, of suspense, of climax and resolution. If the words are fully dramatic, or create all the necessary emotion, they will leave nothing for the music to do. For this reason, the final scene here, the reunion of Jane and Mr Rochester, can be no more than a suggestive sketch. At this point the music must take over, finding a resolution not simply of the dramatic situation but, in the richest possible way, of the musical material, which here reaches its own fulfilment. Words, at this point, had better make themselves scarce and leave that other language, which *can* be dense, in which so many things can be said simultaneously, to get on with it.

April 2000

ACT ONE

Jane in a plain black dress is seated downstage
at her needlework.

JANE

Silence. Quietness.
Some of us choose,
when storms rock the air,
and the wind out on the moor shakes
the wainscot, rattles the pane, a place
of the still heart, out of
the world's eye and the sky's
perpetual knocking.

VOICE (MR ROCHESTER)

Jane! Jane!

JANE

In the wind's lee the nest
is safe on its bough.
No print marks the snow,
no terror affrights
the still breast,
no ghost lifts the latch, leaves
its dent in the pillow.

VOICES (*soprano, alto, child, creating the*
sound of wind on the moors, evoking
Thornfield and its mysteries)

JANE

We stop our ears
to the voices that call us
back—

ROCHESTER

Jane! Jane!

Swing shut
the door of our soul
on a place that is windless,
soundless, remote
from the world's wreck, where days
are calm, no storm unsettles
the nest, no wintry blast
makes tremble the snowdrop.

Jane lays her work aside.

Is it a year, is it just a year
since I set my work aside,
made all tidy,
packed, put on my bonnet

*She rises, puts on a cloak and bonnet, takes
up a bag.*

and left my old self sitting,
to go, all eager,
my breast in a turmoil, to meet
life, fate, my one
true love.

Jane! Jane!

Yes, perhaps
my one true love
in this world and all others,
and came in snowy twilight

VOICES (*evoking Thornfield*)

to the big door of the big
house out on the moor,
Thornfield, Thornfield,
and knocked – and stood there
in the snow, all my girl's heart
beating.

*The door opens. Mrs Fairfax, the housekeeper
at Thornfield, a neat, refined person in her
early fifties.*

JANE

I am expected, I think.

ROCHESTER

Jane. Jane.

MRS FAIRFAX

Miss Eyre?

JANE

Jane Eyre.

ROCHESTER

Jane. Jane.

MRS FAIRFAX

Welcome to Thornfield,
Miss Eyre. On behalf
of the master of this house,
Mr Rochester, welcome
I am his cousin, Mrs Fairfax. I keep
house for him. In his name,
welcome, my dear.

ADELE (*at first offstage*)
Is that Miss Eyre? Is it her
at last? Is she come? Is that
Miss Eyre?

MRS FAIRFAX
And this, Miss Eyre, is Adele,
Mr Rochester's ward –
your charge.

Jane and the child approach one another,
shyly. Jane puts out her hand, Adele runs to
her. Hand in hand they move downstage, Mrs
Fairfax watching a moment, then going off.

ADELE

I can sing you know,
Miss Eyre. *And* dance. Look! (*she dances*)
My mother was a dancer
at the Paris opera.
Mr Rochester, you know, was in love
with her. Miss Eyre, do you know
the mad scene in *Lucia*?

*As Adele begins to sing she is joined offstage
by the voice of Mrs Rochester singing her own
version of madness.*

JANE

What a strange house this is!
Walking today with Mrs Fairfax
in the long gallery under the roof
I heard, from one of the locked rooms,
laughter, a woman's low
laugh, dark as molasses –
Are there ghosts
in this house?
I heard someone laugh behind
that door – a woman's
laugh, dark as molasses.

Adele breaks off, Mrs Rochester continues.

ADELE

Poor Lucia. She killed
her husband, you know,
on the first night, in their marriage bed,
    and went
singing like a ghost
in her bloodsoaked gown – mad!

JANE

Tell me, Adele –
Mr Rochester, is he kind to you?

7

ADELE

Oh yes, he is very kind. He gives me
presents. But he is sad, very sad,
you know. He is always
sad, and sometimes angry.

JANE

With you?

ADELE

Oh no. Just angry. He sits alone
in his room and frowns – like this.
He gives me presents and I love him,
but he is wounded, here
in his heart.

JANE

His heart?

ADELE

Oh yes, he does have a heart, I know
he does, but it is wounded.
That is why he cannot stay with us,
why he is here
one day, then gone.

*Adele goes back to her singing, this time in
French, a little waltz. Slowly she moves off.*

JANE (*alone*)

I have asked myself a thousand times,
what is he like, what is he like, this man
whose house I live in, whose things
are everywhere about us –
this chair he sits in, these books
he reads. Why is he driven
to wander to far places
away from his own home?
Is there something here

at Thornfield that torments him,
that haunts, and torments, so that his heart
    knows no quiet,
can discover no rest?

*Suddenly the sound of a horse's neighing and
Jane is startled by the shadow of a rearing
horse. She falls, looks about. The voices of
Thornfield, including now a man's voice. She
rises, composes herself, goes upstage to where
Mr Rochester stands facing the fireplace. He
turns: his arm is in a sling.*

ROCHESTER

Ah, Miss Eyre, there you are.
So it was you
out there, on the ice, that frightened
my horse and sent me sprawling.
It is to you I owe
this wound. Well, how do you find me,
now I have come at last?
Am I – handsome?

JANE

No, sir, you are not. I mean—

ROCHESTER

So, I disappoint you.
I fail to live up
to your young girl's fantasies.

JANE

I have no fantasies, sir.

ROCHESTER

No fantasies? None?
Oh Miss Eyre, have you not heard that I am
moody, that my nature
is dark, that I have spoiled
my youth in dissipation? Have you not heard
what an ogre I am?

JANE

Sir, I was too plain. I meant only,
Mr Rochester, that beauty
is of no consequence.

ROCHESTER

Of course it is! –
Ah, what eyes you have,
Miss Eyre. To search into a man's
innermost thoughts.

JANE

I mean, sir, that you are stern,
very stern, and your sternness has
a power beyond beauty.
I think you like
to think yourself an ogre.
Out of pride. Out of some
hurt to your affections.

ROCHESTER

And what do you know,
Miss Eyre, Jane Eyre, of my
affections? You have no knowledge
of the world and its evil.

JANE

I know, sir, you are unhappy.
I know there is something in this place—

ROCHESTER

You mean the world?

JANE

I mean this house, I mean Thornfield—
(VOICES)
that haunts you, drives you away
from hearth and home and those here
who love you.

ROCHESTER

And are there those in this house
who love me? I tell you,
Miss Eyre, I tell you,
Jane, Jane, I love this house,
its thorn trees, its old façade,
its windows, darkly ablaze,
but to me it is a plague house
to be shunned. Always, always at the door
of Thornfield there stands

11

a figure that bars my way,
a hag who raises
her finger, and with that finger writes in the
    air
Love it if you can, Edward Rochester,
Come home if you dare—
and laughs!

Towards the end of this the figure of Mrs
Rochester appears, her hair wild, in a night-
gown. She holds up her finger and writes. She
laughs. Her laughter, crazy, over rising music:
flames and a hint of something Caribbean.
Jane and Mr Rochester recede. The woman
dances. Flames. Mr Rochester reappears. She
hurls herself at him and involves him in her
dance, he struggles, gets away, but his face is
scratched. He beats at the flames. Jane
appears in her nightgown.

JANE

Mr Rochester, you are hurt.

ROCHESTER

No, It is nothing. A little blood.

JANE

You're bleeding. Who has done this?
Your face is torn as if
some savage beast—

ROCHESTER

And you Jane, you—

JANE

Untouched, unharmed.
But who has done this to you?
Who spread these flames? Who tore
your face? What savage beast—

ROCHESTER

Did you see no one,
Jane? Did you hear no one?

JANE

No, sir, no one. But I heard
laughter. I have heard
that laughter before. From behind
a locked door, a woman's
laugh, dark as molasses.

ROCHESTER

Jane, Jane, let this night's horrors
be a secret between us. Ask no more.
Come here, Jane, come out here
where there is some freshness
to the air, away from the smell
of ashes. The house is like a dungeon,
don't you feel it?

13

JANE

I heard laughter. I have heard
that laughter before, a woman's
laugh, dark as molasses.

ROCHESTER

Here Jane, will you have a flower?
Let us forget this night, all that madness
of fury and flames. Here is a flower,
so pure, look at the order
of it, the simplicity.
And listen. The birds
are waking, bringing their young ones
food. After such a night,
Jane, there is the day!
Look at me, Jane –
ah, what eyes you have,
Jane, Jane Eyre, to search into a man's
innermost thoughts.
Listen now, I shall tell you
a story. Imagine
a boy, wild in his nature,
from his first childhood spoiled.
See him, a youth not twenty,
alone among strangers, far
from home on an island
of hot days, hotter nights, in the West Indies.
Conceive that he commits
there a fatal error – not a crime,
no, not a crime but such
an error as might taint
a man's whole existence
with horror and filth – O the years, the long
years and misery of it, the sun at noon
darkened, and on the soul
a weight never lifted.

JANE

Whose story is this? Why does my blood

14

quicken so, with pity,
with fear? Is this the story
I sought? Is it my life now that the story
demands for its end?
Is this the door
that opened when I came, my young girl's
   heart
beating, and knocked at the door
of the big house on the moor,
Thornfield?

ROCHESTER

Heart weary, soul-embittered, he
comes home after long absence,
to the big house on the moor,
Thornfield, and there, in the place
of darkness there is light, there is promise
of new life.

JANE

But I know this story.
I have heard it in my soul. It is my own
story. This is the story
my whole life has been telling!

ROCHESTER

After twenty years, a moment
without taint or soil. Daybreak!
Oh Jane, Jane, you almost unearthly creature,
I love you. Will you be mine? Say yes
quickly, before the shadows
close in once more about me.

JANE

Quietness. Quietness.
Some of us choose
when storms rock the air
and the wind out on the moor shakes
the wainscot, rattles the pane, a place

of the still heart –

ROCHESTER
Jane, Jane,
say it. Say Edward – give me my name –
Say, Edward, yes,
yes, I will marry you.

JANE
Yes, Edward, yes, I will marry you.

ROCHESTER
(turning away towards the house)
Who now will deny me? Who will say
I have no right to this?
To leap over stale custom
and convention! To have the life
at last of an immortal being!
    (Woman's laughter)

Jane has to call him back to reality.

JANE
Sir, Mr Rochester, Edward, I said
yes.

ROCHESTER
Jane, Jane. Let me hold you, Jane,
you're trembling. But we are safe. Look
it is daylight. There is nothing
to fear.

ACT II

*Jane seated on her bed. A full-length looking
glass. Mrs Fairfax and Adele enter, Mrs
Fairfax carrying Jane's wedding veil. The
dress already hangs, rather ghostlike, on a
model nearby.*

MRS FAIRFAX
Jane, my dear, it has come.
Your veil.

ADELE
(*Taking and holding it up*)
It's so beautiful. Look.
(*She dances round with it*)

MRS FAIRFAX
The child wants to sing you
a little song, my dear. To wish you
health and happiness
in your new life. (*Adele begins to sing*)
You have brought so much joy to us,
Jane – to us, and to Thornfield,
and to him, Mr Rochester.

ADELE
(*As she sings she crowns Jane with the veil.
Jane goes to the looking-glass to examine her
image*)

So pure, as white as water,
as soft as mist, as pale
as light, this bridal veil
will shield the bride of Thornfield
tonight. Let nothing evil
approach. Let no wish fail.
Upon her health and fortune,
for ever softly fall.

JANE

I can scarcely believe it.
It is a dream. I can scarcely believe
it's me. The bride
of Thornfield. Jane
Eyre. Tomorrow to be
another. His wife. Mrs Rochester.

*Further back Mrs Rochester appears as Jane
turns to the mirror.*

MRS ROCHESTER

She the bride of Thornfield?
Mrs Rochester? Who am I
then? Who am I? A ghost
in this house? Oh Edward, Edward –
why have you put me
away? Why have you sent me
to a living grave? Condemned me
to walk the corridors
of this house, a living
ghost? Mrs Edward Rochester, the ghost
of Thornfield.

*Jane takes off the veil, hangs it beside the
dress. Mrs Fairfax and Adele prepare to leave
her.*

MRS FAIRFAX/ADELE

Goodnight, my dear. Goodnight,
Miss Eyre, for the last time,
Miss Eyre. Jane, God bless you.
Let nothing evil
approach. Goodnight. Goodnight.

*Jane sleeps. Mrs Rochester comes forward.
She takes the veil. Places it on her head.
Stands a moment, quietly looking at herself in
the glass. Slowly she begins to dance, at first*

lightly, then more sensuously, then madly.
Wordlessly singing. At last she screams and
begins to tear at the veil. Jane wakes. Mrs
Rochester and Jane face one another a
moment in silence. Mrs Rochester raises her
hand. A knife. Both women freeze. Jane
screams. Mr Rochester enters, unseen by Jane.
He too stands perfectly still, Mrs Rochester
still with the knife raised in one hand, the torn
veil raised high in the other. Slowly she lowers
the knife under his gaze.

JANE

Who are you?

MRS ROCHESTER
(*to Jane*) Who am I? Who am I, Edward?

JANE
(*who realises now that Mr Rochester is also*
present)
Edward, Edward, who is this woman?

MRS ROCHESTER
Edward. Who am I?
Mrs Rochester! I am Mrs
Edward Rochester,
the bride of Thornfield.

Grandly she turns, sweeping the veil about
her, and walks off.

JANE
Oh sir, is this true?
Is that unhappy woman
what I was to be tomorrow –
your wife, Mrs Rochester?

21

ROCHESTER

Oh Jane, Jane, give me my name
again, call me Edward. But you cannot know
what a fiend she is!
You saw how she tore my face –
a wild beast you called her.

JANE

I had not seen her then.
Now I have seen her.
Your wife Edward;
in this world and the next
your one and only wife,
Edward.

ROCHESTER

And you, Jane?

JANE

I, sir? I?
I am Jane Eyre. I
am Jane Eyre, Jane Eyre.

ROCHESTER

Jane you must listen to me.
Have you no pity?

JANE

Yes, I have pity, I have pity –
for your wife, that poor mad woman.
And for myself who was to be
your wife and will remain
myself now, Jane Eyre, since I love you,
and only you.

ROCHESTER

And me, Jane, have you no pity
for *me*? Only you can save me,
Jane. Would you see me bound

for ever to that mad woman, that fiend, for all
eternity bound, flesh to flesh
without joy, without love, without one word
of comfort, through all eternity?

JANE

She is your wife.
What can I be
to you? I must go from here –
and quickly. From you,
Edward, and from Thornfield—

ROCHESTER

Jane, I never meant
to harm you. I wanted only
to give you happiness,
that small gift. And after
twenty years of torment to grasp
some comfort of my own.

JANE

And what of her? What of your wife,
Edward? She cannot help it that she is mad.

ROCHESTER

Jane, Jane, it is not her madness
I hate. Do you think, Jane, if you
were mad that I would hate you?
Listen, Jane. Hear the rest
of my tale. I was twenty, wild,
foolish, a spoiled boy
of twenty.
(*Behind we see a young Mrs Rochester.*
Seductive dance, which slowly becomes
wanton – she eases the dress off her shoulders,
is at last bare-breasted. Makes wild gestures.
Shakes out her hair. A mad woman.)
All Spanish Town knew what she was.
I was betwitched

by her beauty. All my senses on that island
of hot days, hotter nights
afire with her skin, her eyes, her tainted lips,
her laugh, dark as molasses.
I was their fool! Only later did I learn
my father knew their secret.
He sold me for the dowry!
Thirty thousand
pounds we were sold for, she and I,
I and that poor mad girl, now a mad
woman, forever bound, flesh to flesh
she in her world
of delirium and vileness,
I in my long
passion and punishment of living
bound to this mad woman,
in shame and secrecy.
And then, Jane, then, one afternoon, I rode
again towards Thornfield,
as always dreading what I must find there,
    and found
you, Jane, my good angel—

JANE

Sir, this is madness. I must go—

ROCHESTER

You mean to leave me?

JANE

I do. I do.

ROCHESTER

(*clasps her*) And still?

JANE

I do.

24

ROCHESTER
(*kissing her*) And still? Jane! Jane!

JANE
(*breaking from him*)
Forgive me. We shall meet again,
Edward, I do believe that, and long for it,
    but not
in this world—

ROCHESTER
Jane. Jane. Does my deep love,
my deeper woe not move you?

JANE
My love, my dear love, never again, never,
    never
in this world. I am going. Do not break
my heart by calling to me.

She begins to walk downstage. He walks
slowly backward into the shadows.

Jane moves downstage to where we first
found her. Sits.

MR ROCHESTER
Jane. Jane.

Jane takes up her needlework.

MRS ROCHESTER
(*appears*) Edward

Mr Rochester and the mad woman in a deadly
struggle lit by flames. Voices of Rochester,
Mrs Rochester, Mrs Fairfax, Adele, the voices
of Thornfield, but transformed, chaotic.

MR ROCHESTER
Jane, Jane, where are you, Jane?

JANE
(*same words as opening, but urgent now,
hysterical*)
Silence. Quietness. Some of us choose
when storms rock the air
quietness. Quietness.

*The fire music rises to a climax, Mrs
Rochester falling in flames. Rochester trying
to save her by beating out the flames, his face
blackened with ashes.*

JANE
We stop our ears
to the voices that call us
back. My love, my dear love, never
again, never, never
in this world. I am Jane
Eyre. I am Jane Eyre.
Jane Eyre.

*Mr Rochester struggles free of the ruins,
blind, holding his hands out before him.*

ROCHESTER
Jane! Jane! Where are you,
my angel? I am in the dark!
Free but alone and imprisoned in the dark.
Jane! Jane!

*Jane puts her work down. Listens. The
whirling of wind. Thornfield. Far off his
voice, calling.*

ROCHESTER
Jane!

*Music falls. Jane rises. Listening. Slowly as the
music for the final scene begins, moves upstage
to where Mr Rochester is waiting, his arms
outstretched. She runs the last steps. They
embrace.*

ROCHESTER

Jane. Jane. Is it really you?
Are you real? I called to you out of the dark.
I am blind, Jane. Are you real?
Is it you? Have you answered out of
the dark and come to me?
Jane, Jane, you must never leave me.

JANE

It is Jane, Edward. It is Jane.
I have come, I have answered you out of
the dark, I have come
to you, my love, my dear love.
I will not leave you
again, my love, my dear love.
Never again, never, never
in this world. Never. Never.